The Necronaut

THE NECRONAUT

R. N. JORDEN

Denver, Colorado

Published in the United States by:
Spaceboy Books LLC
1627 Vine Street
Denver, CO 80206
www.readspaceboy.com

First printed April 2017

ISBN-10:
0-9987120-2-7

ISBN-13:
978-0-9987120-2-4

For Bobbi, who joined a New Wave band
Changed her name to Bobbi Sox
Eloise, who played guitar,
Sang songs about whales and cops
Terri who didn't give a shit
Was just a nihilist
And Ronnie who was much more my style
Cause she wrote songs just like this.

1. Tang wasn't the only thing they took.

The helmet is supposed to make a loud *click-woosh* when it's sealed properly, allowing the flight suit to generate the pilot's personal atmosphere. She thought she'd heard it click, but it wasn't like a *click-click*; more of a *thud*.

Then again, maybe that's how it always sounded.

Then again, again, she'd attached this helmet hundreds of times, and she didn't remember questioning the sound before.

So, while she had a second, she detached the helmet. There was a hollow pop as the oxygen released from the suit into the cockpit. She took a deep breath from the still pressurized cabin and re-attached the helmet.

Click-woosh.

She was more satisfied with the *click* that time, but thought the *woosh* wasn't quite right.

Pop.

Click-woosh.

She was sure she could hear air hissing out from the collar.

Pop.

Click-woosh.

Was it still hissing?

Pop.

Click-woosh.

```
—y-seconds    until    launch,    Karen.    Is
something wrong with your helmet interlock?
```

"Huh? No. I don't think so. Why?"

```
The display keeps cycling between PLS on
and PLS off. You sure nothing's wrong?
```

"Not as far as I know."

She resisted the urge to remove the helmet again.

Huh. Well, you'd better self-test, just in
case.

Karen reached up and double-tapped the diagnostic key
just above the helmet's visor. Pleasantly modulated synth-
speech replaced the flight director's nasal, North Eastern accent
in her helmet's speakers.

Good morning, MAJOR KELLER. The primary
life support system is active and functioning
normally. Your current body temperature is
ninety-seven point nine degrees Fahrenheit. Your
current heart rate is—

"I think we've heard enough from my hat today" she
said, tapping the diagnostic routine off. She was worried the
heart rate monitor would reveal how nervous she was. Or, the
copious amount of pre-flight amphetamines she'd ingested.

Pop.

Click-woosh.

2. The Maryland state motto, but, you know, backwards.

When Major Keller was still a minor, she lived with her folks in a log cabin in Telluride, Colorado. That was how her mother referred to it. Really, though, it was a log cabin in the same way that the Vietnam War was a "police action." Karen's childhood home was a ten thousand square-foot, tree adorned mansion. Her father once described it as "if some Ewoks won the lottery and tried to gentrify Endor." Karen's mother, neither knowing nor caring what Ewoks were, kissed him patronizingly on the forehead and went jogging.

So, the house was really big. We're getting to why, scooter. Settle down.

Ernest Jerome "Ernie" Keller and Kate Louise Mason "Mase"-Keller had both achieved a certain level of celebrity and success that afforded them their wooden fortress. For comparison's sake, here are two distinct headlines about them:

"Local Entrepreneur Ernie Keller creates purr-fect fashion line for pampered pets"—*The Telluride Daily Planet,* **April 30, 2097**

Now, let's not diminutize Ernie's cat sweater breakthroughs, as he did sell a shitload of them. But there was a *slightly* bigger one for his wife:

"USMC-NASA astronaut Mason-Keller returns from first manned trans-dimensional flight" *—The Washington Post,* **November 20, 2097**

Twenty ninety-seven was a big year for the Kellers, for physicists, and for pets that get chilly easily.

3. Wired

She was aware of the countdown in her headset, even if she wasn't listening to it. Truth be told, actively listening was irrelevant; the ship would launch at t minus zero whether she heard it or not. She couldn't back out now, no matter how hard her teeth were chattering. Resetting her jaw and clenching it tight, she swiveled her head around the cramped cockpit. She hoped that focusing on the lights and gauges would take her mind off all of the things that could go wrong, but really she just gave the displays the same of kind of cursory glances that someone would a menu when they weren't really hungry. Also, she wasn't one hundred percent on what all of them were, or what they represented.

"It's fine," Colonel Morrison had explained to Karen in the hangar, with her raspy, mannish voice. "These new ships, they basically fly themselves. Goddamn near idiot-proof. Not only that," the Colonel rapped on the side of the white-ish hull of one of the ships "this is Mase's bird. Even if you don't have any of her" Morrison looked Karen up-and-down, pausing ever so briefly at her waistline "you'll at least have her equipment."

Karen looked up from her shoes just in time to see a helmet hurtling toward her chest. She reached out to catch it, but it jammed the middle finger on her left hand, she yelped, and a hundred and fifty thousand taxpayer dollars clattered to the polished floor.

Ignoring Morrison's theatrical groan, Karen picked up the helmet by the bottom of the full-face visor, with her left hand. The helmet, like the ship, was presumably bright white at one point, but now a little dinged up and sort of dingy; they both also had "Captain Katherine 'Mase' Mason" stenciled nicely upon them. As Karen rotated the helmet around, a cable tumbled out and hung a few inches from the floor.

"What's that? For headphones or something?"

Morrison took the helmet from Karen and detached the cabling from inside the helmet. "No, that'd be a neural uploader. They were supposed to take it out."

"What do—"

"Ah, it was like a, without getting too technical, it uploaded information; brain activity and such, from the pilot to the craft, in case—well, never mind. We don't use them anymore. Waste of time and money. They're gonna retrofit the helmet for your head anyhow."

"Can't I just have my own?"

"Negative. The helmet is synced to the craft. They both operate at the optimum. Plus, we need to eliminate as many variables as possible."

Karen felt a little woozy and sat on a steel crate. "Man, I, I don't know about all this."

The Colonel walked over and slapped Karen on the back hard enough to make her cough. "Ah, you'll be fine. Besides, you're Mase's daughter. You've got flying in your blood."

Besides a bit of methamphetamine, a somewhat alarming lack of iron due to an aversion to eating animal products, and researching a healthy diet to make up for it, there wasn't anything special about her blood, Karen thought. Definitely not some kind of genetic memory for flying spacecraft. Or, for anything military, really. She wasn't terribly close to her mother, especially after her mother returned from her inter-dimensional excursion a babbling wreck and burned down a children's hospital.

She really got along with her dad, though.

T-minus five.

4. The economy of truth

The absorption of NASA by the Marine Corps had its pros and cons. The pro-est of which was an infusion of capital. The nearly broke and on the verge of being dissolved space administration could suddenly draw from an operations budget that was actually funded. For that, there was much rejoicing and an agency-wide party. The newly full coffers afforded three full-sized sheet cakes, only one of which had a brutal misspelling on it. Still, everyone agreed that "Congratulations Nassau" was just as delicious as the other two, and it was German chocolate.

On the con-ish side: the NASA scientists' normal predilection towards telling everyone about something they discovered in long, arduous detail, had to be curtailed a bit by folks with starched uniforms and severe haircuts. The Marine Corps, known for playing things a bit closer to the vest, had an institutional opposition to releasing unadulterated statements. So Doctor Kendrick's report reading "Seventh successful manned mission proves unequivocally that what is colloquially known 'The Afterlife' is a real and tangible place, accessible via trans-dimensional wormhole" became Colonel Morrison's begrudgingly released headline to *The Washington Post.*

"It's not lying, Doctor" the Colonel said. "We're simply being economical with the truth. Now, run along and stop pouting."

Doctor Kendrick did not stop pouting. Instead, he continued to complain loudly about the situation to anyone he thought could even be remotely useful.

He would later die via thirty-six gunshot wounds to the head and chest, self-inflicted.

5. Things get heavy

Karen snapped into attention at t-minus two. She'd managed to ride out the jittery overture of the amphetamines, and made it to the solid shore of intense focus. People forget that most drugs had therapeutic use before people had the audacity to just start taking them for fun. Karen's use was mostly the former. She was merely upholding a long tradition of humans hurtling through air and space, tweaked out of their eyeballs.

Seriously, look it up sometime. You'll be shocked at how literally and figuratively high our pilots and astronauts have been.

Unfortunately, for Karen, it wasn't the best time to be unusually cognizant. The actual launch was totally automated, so she had nothing to do except bury her fingers into the undersides of the seat's armrests while the compartment swayed from the power of the engines igniting. She was more aware than she'd have liked of every bit of pressure clamping her against the seat back. The craft was small and not built with comfort in mind. She could feel every vibration from its rigid hull, through the floor, up her legs, and into her back teeth.

"It's like flying a tuning fork at nineteen-thousand miles an hour" Karen remembered her mother telling her father, seemingly in order to break his balls about his complaint that their riding lawnmower was "kinda uncomfortable." Mase had a fifth degree black belt in one-upmanship. Karen thought of her mother; her sharp, hawkish features probably unmoved by the strains of the launch. Karen, on the other hand, had a fairly average fullness to her face, most of which seemed to have run back behind her jawline to escape the punishing g-forces. She grabbed the armrests tighter, hoping that she wouldn't be completely liquefied.

Eight-and-one half minutes later, she exceeded escape velocity. Freed from the tyranny of gravity, she looked over her shoulder and waved bye, just in case.

6. Bucket Seats

Major Mason-Keller made all seven successful trans-dimensional flights. You'll notice that the word "flights" came with a qualifier.

After her first successful trip, all other exploratory projects were suspended, with all available assets diverted to "determining the feasibility of establishing a forward operations center in Section Bravo 42." In English: the Marines wanted to put military bases in the afterlife. After all, that's the reason they absorbed NASA in the first place; so they could send scouts to find tactically advantageous spots in every galaxy and possible reality.

To date, only Mase had found one and it was a fucking doozy.

But one was enough. It was certainly enough to petition congress for emergency funding. Luckily, the head of the committee in charge of funding the newly-christened USMCNASA was the senior senator from North Carolina, whose state housed Zimmerman-Dylan Dynamics. ZDD was responsible for the design and manufacture of the single-person *Danvers* class spacecraft. Of course, building ten more would require a few hundred new workers hired. So, win-win.

Well, mostly win-win. The cake budget was summarily suspended, pending an anti-trust investigation.

In the time it took for the rest of the ships to be finished, Mase had made two more successful trips. Successful in that she survived them, but wildly unsuccessful as none of her recording or analytic equipment had come back intact from either trip. Her verbal debriefings were so ethereal and bordering on insane, that they were classified into absolute oblivion. Major Mason-Keller was placed on administrative leave, as her psych evaluations were beginning to be overrun with question marks and the word "concerning."

The next person through the wormhole was an older Marine, a veteran of two wars and three space flights. His name was Captain Douglas Moore, and he took off for Bravo 42 from a semi-secret facility in Lamoni, Iowa. He entered and exited the wormhole at the exact same moment, as it was normally perceived by mission control. The craft returned without a scratch, but with no useable data, and malfunctioning sensor arrays. Captain Moore didn't respond, and his craft was brought down remotely.

One of the crash team responders hopped up and pulled the emergency cockpit releases. Upon seeing the thick, grayish-tan puddle that used to be Doug Moore, he threw up. The crash team spent the next three hours sopping up the mixture of pilot and vomit with various blankets and the shirts off their backs. The seats in the *Danvers* class ships were concave in such a way, thankfully, that most of Doug (and all of the vomit) stayed collected in it. The disparate, sopping wet remains of Doug were placed into a vacuum sealed bag and given to the lab at Lamoni, for analysis.

Captain Douglas Moore was reported missing and presumed lost at sea, during a training accident. He was given a closed casket funeral, which was just as well, as it would have probably been even tougher on his loved ones to see an open coffin filled with crusty blankets and undershirts.

After the incident, the crash team was outfitted with a medically sterile, twenty-gallon wet/dry vac. It ended up seeing a lot of action.

7. Well, Neil Armstrong's speech was prepared.

"This is so fucking boring" Karen muttered, less than two minutes after reaching space. She'd been through two-hundred simulated flights, and listened to almost as many dinner table stories from her mother about the wonders of the cosmos, that the real thing lacked any kind of real punch.

Repeat, Major.

"Huh?"

Please repeat your last transmission.

"I said, this is—" she paused. "It's not important. I didn't realize the mic was on." She started to feel a little twitchy, wondering if all her speed-induced fidgeting had turned it on by mistake.

All of the recording systems engage automatically when the launch starts. We need to make sure we get everything we can, in case—

"In case I melt."

Well, it's not technically melting since
that's a reaction to heat. The technical term is
soluble discorporation. But you really don't have
to worry about that, all the tests went fine.

Karen rolled her eyes so hard that she feared the sheer
force would blow her helmet off. "I don't know if sending a jar
of my fingernail and hair clippings through space is a good
enough test that I want to bet my insolubility on it."

Colonel Morrison's husky alto replaced the flight
controllers voice.

Major, all necessary precautions have been
taken. Please refrain from clogging up the comms
with sarcastic asides and profane muttering.

"Can you just call me Karen?" she sighed, already
prescient of the answer.

No, Major, I cannot. You are piloting a
military vessel, and you will be addressed with a
military rank.

"Calling it piloting is a bit of a stretch. Everything's
automatic, there's nothing to really do."

That's good. Gives you plenty of time to
get over how fucking bored you are, and learn to
appreciate the majesty of the goddamned universe.

8. Houses in motion

On January 3, 2104 Karen Keller received the first and only physical letter she'd ever actually seen. It was a rectangle roughly the size of a small media tablet, printed on actual paper; delivered by a thoroughly unremarkable man in a serious-looking uniform. It read:

The President of the United States,

To: Ms. Karen Ernest KELLER
2236-B Ten Apple Drive,
Telluride, CO, 81435

Greetings,

You are hereby ordered for induction into the Armed Forces of the United States, and to report at 1715 REPUBLIC AVENUE, CORVALLIS, OREGON – 3RD FLOOR

on 8 JANUARY at 7:25 am

for forwarding to an Armed Forces Induction Station.

She stood on her front porch in tattered pajama pants and a hooded sweatshirt that bordered on enormous, reading and re-reading the notice. She was so engrossed that she didn't notice the courier waving, getting frustrated by her lack of response, then aggressively giving her the double bird before he returned to his truck. She flipped the page over, saw that it was blank, then flipped back. She understood all of the words in a vacuum, but couldn't grasp them bunched together in the order presented in the letter.

To be fair, she was the only person to be conscripted into the United States Military in a hundred and thirty years, and the very idea of being drafted was so far out of the cultural consciousness that most history curriculums (curricula, if you're an asshole) didn't even bother mentioning it. She lamented the notice not having digital info links.

Paper, as it turned out, wasn't terribly clickable. So, she did what we all do when we need to know about old, boring, useless shit.

She walked up the hill to her folks' house.

9. Substitute Corpses

Karen's parents' front door was so unbelievably heavy that her mother had to have a micro-hydraulic system custom built into the antique hinges, to facilitate the doors' opening by anyone whose name wasn't immediately followed by "champion of the worrrrld," and afterwards didn't get any less intimidating. Painstaking reproductions of famous statues in perfectly spaced rows sat dust free atop an incredibly intricate herringbone nuWood floor. Mase tried to drill the names of the statues into her daughter's mind, but the only thing she succeeded on was convincing Karen that "Our Lady of Cardigan" was not an appropriate place to hang her jacket.

Karen made her way to the base of the spiral stairs only to be scared one-eighth shitless by a staccato, metallic voice emanating from nowhere in particular.

Hello, KAREN KELLER. How may I assist you?

"Jesus Christ! I don't know!"

KAREN KELLER, your voice indicates you are in distress. Would you like me to contact someone?

"Uh, my dad?"

I'm sorry. I seem to be having trouble
understanding you. Please re—

"Daaaaaaaaaaaaaaaaaad!!!"

I'm sorry. I appear to be—

"Oh my God, shut up! Dad!"

Karen felt a tug at her sleeve. She turned around to find
all five feet and seven inches of her father giving her the one
finger "hush" gesture.

Hello, ERNEST KELLER. Your daughter, KAREN
KELLER has entered the premises. Would you like
me to alert CAPTAIN MASON-KELLER?

The awful, over modulated voice asked at such a volume
that the individual panes of glass rattled in the windows
throughout the house.

"Well, not really, but I think it might be moot."

Muting.

"That's not wh— never mind, that's fine" her father said,
pushing up his glasses so he could pinch the bridge of his nose.

"Sooo, what brings you back to the nest, baby bird?" he
asked, dropping down to sit on the staircase.

"This." Karen shoved the paper towards her father's face. He took it from her, and returned his glasses to their effective position.

"Keller...induction...Corvallis—Scooter, this is a draft notice."

"A what?"

"Have a sit" he said, patting the step where he sat.

"Eh, I'm alright. What's this paper now?"

Ernie sighed. "Okay, so, way back; like a hundred years ago back, armies used to have these great, big-ass ground wars. Like, with a bunch of people on foot shooting at each other. That's where the phrase 'boots on the ground' comes from."

"What?"

"Never mind. Anyway, these armies were humongous. So, they needed like, shitloads of people. But, they had a hard time filling out these armies, mostly because no one wants to get shot. Also, the people who didn't mind getting shot often got shot, so they'd have to back-fill those spots. Since no one wants to be a substitute corpse, governments would send out notices like" he shook the paper in his hand "to tell people they had to join the military."

"Yeah, that sounds like it sucks. What does that have to do with me? We're not at war—" she glanced furtively around for an open newsscan. "Are we?"

"Not as of this morning."

"Soooo..."

Her father shrugged. "Sooo, I'm not sure" he said, searching for some bit of wisdom to impart to his daughter. "You want to smoke a joint with your old man?" is what he landed on.

"Of course I do."

10. It's a Flat Circle

The wormhole, such as it was, didn't have an entryway on the visible spectrum. Even if it had, Karen was too busy chewing on the inside of her cheek and counting the number of indicator lights on the ship's control panel to notice it. The only reason she looked up at all was

```
    Attention, MAJOR KELLER. We are entering
the Bravo 42 anomaly. Please brace yourself for
trans-dimensional incursion.
```

```
    Oh, and
```

```
    Alright, Major. This is it. Rem—
```

The transmission ended abruptly. Karen assumed the colonel was going to say "remember," but she also could have imagined her saying "remain." That said, she wasn't sure what she was supposed to remember or remain, so it didn't matter much.

"Well, looks like we've heard enough from Colonel Morrison today. How're we doing?"

```
    The craft's hull is at one-hundred percent
integrity. Propulsion systems are on standby and
```

the craft is currently propelled what you would
perceive as 'forward' by the intrinsic inertia
created by the anomaly. Your curren—

"Wait. Explain 'perceive as forward.'" Karen said, feeling
like someone probably explained it to her already.

Apologies, MAJOR. The anomaly does not
conform to the restraints of the three spatial
dimensions. Therefore, 'forward' can only be used
as a means of communicating progression.

"So how is that any different from anywhere else in
space?"

There are established means of navigating
in space: The Galactic Coordinate system, right
ascension/declination and the like. There are
also established points of reference in space.
None of those things are applicable within the
anomaly, nor beyond it.

"And the thing is pulling us through on its own."

Affirmative.

"So, what if I want to turn around and go back?"

Propulsion systems are non-functional within the
anomaly. 'Turning around' is non-feasible.

"Why?" Karen asked, feeling blood run across her tongue from where she'd clamped down on her cheek harder.

With no point of navigational reference, orientation is an impossibility. The anomaly's inertia cannot be interrupted. The concept of 'back' cannot be established within the anomaly.

"Oh, well that's fucking tremendous. It'd have been nice if someone explained all this shit to me before we left."

Replaying mission briefing from twenty-second Janu-

"Yeah, whatever" she cut the ship off. She reached up to take off her helmet, but was herself cut off by a piercing klaxon and a stern reprimand.

MAJOR KELLER, PLS interruption is not permitted for the duration of the mission. If you would like your personal atmosphere adjusted, please vocalize your request.

"Fucking fine. How long will it be before we get to Bravo 42 proper."

Indeterminable.

"Explain."

Gravity cannot be ascertained within the
anomaly. Due to the factors mentioned earlier,
calculating velocity of any type within the
anomaly is impossible. There is no fixed point to
measure to, nor does time function within the
anomaly in a way that is linearly comprehensible.

"So, could be ten minutes, could be a hundred years."

Affirmative.

Karen resisted the urge to yelp as one of her canine teeth
punched all the way through her cheek.

11. Pass

"Thi-*whuff*-s tastes...weird. Like, I don't know, dirt?"

Her father took the expertly rolled joint from her, and took three sharp inhales.

"Tastes fi-*hrrrk*-fine to me. Natural, from the Earth. The way it should be" he held it between his thumb and index finger, examining it thoughtfully before handing it back.

"Eh, the ones from the store are better. They don-*whuff*-they, uh... shit."

"Well, you're perfectly capable of going to the store and buying some of that chemical-laden garbage."

Karen shook her head. "Unwilling and incapable. I am excitably broke."

Ernie carefully pried the last bit of joint from his daughter's hand. He flopped back on the porch swing where he did all of his smoking, and most of his thinking. Mase wasn't particularly keen on him doing either of those things when he could be doing something "productive." Needless to say, but doing so anyway, he spent more and more time on the porch with each passing day. Karen opened her mouth to continue talking about her current monetary plight, but hit a massive pothole, and decided to just sit on the porch swing too.

"What happened to your allowance?"

"Did you not notice this ensemble?" she asked, waving vaguely in the direction of her sweatshirt. "Fifty-percent cotton blends ain't free, son."

Ernie smiled and laughed. "I guess it's a good thing you're going to be gainfully employed, presently" he said looking back to the draft notice he was still holding. He could feel the corners of his mouth creep back toward their center.

"Yeah," she sighed. "What do you think that's all about?" she waved off the last puff.

"I don't know, Bug. You should probably talk to your mom about it. I'm sure it has something to do with her."

"Pass."

"Don't pass. She's actually been much more lucid lately."

"Oh, well in that case—*Hard* pass."

12. The Great Space Colon

"How long have we been here?"

    Indeterminable.   It   is   impossible   to
calculate the entry ti—

"Right. Yeah. I remember." Karen said, aimlessly looking at the gauges. Many of the ones still functioning that had either changed readings intermittently, or displayed a value like ∞. She wished she had been able to bring movies with her, like she'd wanted, but Colonel Martinet had expressly forbade it. She'd discovered the three films and the portable player that Karen half-assedly hid under the pilot seat.

"Major Keller," she'd growled from behind her desk. "It is *imperative* that you are completely focused on the mission. You are to remain aware and visually note everything about the anomaly, and Bravo 42. Not to mention that your hasty shoving of *Katana Mamas* disconnected the presence sensor for your seat. For that reason" she smirked "You are hereby restricted to your quarters until launch day. Dismissed."

"Can I have my movies back?"

"I had the Maintenance Chief dispose of them. I've also taken the precaution of having all media removed from your quarters. Oh, and please stop at the lab on your way to quarters.

The CMO says he's been hounding you for the last round of fluid samples. *Dismissed.*"

Karen got up from the chair and performed a theatrical bow. On the way down, she spat a small lake's worth of phlegm and saliva onto the Colonel's desk."

"Tell the CMO that he can come scoop that shit up."

"Keller! I'll—"

"You'll what? Get someone else two days before the launch? Oh, wait; there is no one else" she said, kicking the chair over with her heel. "Fuck you, *sir*" she hissed, before making her way back to the quarters where she stayed, stewing for the next forty-three hours.

—or Keller.

"Huh?"

Have you been able to note the visual properties of the anomaly, per mission directives? The craft's exterior optical arrays are non-functional.

Karen looked at the paper notebook and pen strapped to the bulkhead. "Oh, yeah, I'm on top of it."

MAJOR, the interior optical arrays are still functional.

Karen shrugged. "Yeah, so what? There's nothing to note. Outside the ship just looks like a giant blue rectum."

I'm sorry, MAJOR. I'm not sure I understand your point of reference.

"Oh. I guess you wouldn't. Do you know what a colonoscopy is?"

Colonoscopy is a procedure in which a trained specialist uses a long, flexible, narrow tube with a light and tiny camera on one end, called a colonoscope or scope, to observe a rectum and colon. Typically performed on adult males.

"Uh, yeah. So, when I was in high school, my dad got one. After you get one, they send you home with a video of the procedure, so you can give it to your regular doc—wait, why can't they just email the—well, maybe—doesn't matter. Anyway, he left the video in the media console and I watched by accident. It was *super* gross, right? But I could not stop watching it. It was fucking fascinating. So, everyday, for a week or so, I'd get home, smoke a little reefer, and watch this, this tour of my dad's asshole."

Would you like me to use that explanation as the official report on the structure of the anomaly?

"Oh my god yes."

38

13. Family Tradition

Her request to pass rejected, Karen trudged her way up the main staircase to see her mother, the draft notice crumpled in her right hand. Before her mother's brains were boiled by the complications of exploration, she would jog up and down these stairs to stay trim. At four thirty in the morning. *Every* morning, despite the persistent wailing and pillow chucking aimed at the contrary.

Thump-thump-thump-thump- "et est nomen meum Katherine" *thump-thump-thump* "sum in mundo optimum gubernatorem" *thump-thump.*

Oh, and she'd yell-chant custom mantras in other languages.

Just 'cause.

But, again, that was before. These days, Mase's exercise mainly consisted of screaming at her husband and prodigious night terrors. If it'd happened to anyone else, Karen would have felt awful for them. As it stood with her mother, well, she wouldn't go as far as to say that she sort of deserved it, but she'd imply as much.

"Mom! Are you up there?" Karen asked, taking a minute to rest, about twenty steps from the landing. "Moooooooooom?"

No response. She shrugged and turned around to head back down, but her father had already anticipated her gambit, and was ten steps below her, pantomiming pushing her up the stairs.

"You know she's up there, bug. Just go on." he whispered.

"You just go!"

"I just go every day! Go see your mother! Please!"

"Ergh."

"Go!"

Disinterested in the Keller tradition of shouting-whisper fights, Karen turned back and finished the staircase ascent. She padded lightly onto the hall carpet, hoping that her mother was asleep, and that she wouldn't wake her on the way to the door. After all, no one could be angry with her for not rousting her poor, sick, demen—

Hello, CAPTAIN MASON-KELLER, your daughter, KAREN KELLER is on the second floor.

"I don't care" came wafting down the hall, in a tired contralto.

Karen wasn't sure if her mother was already up, or the screamy computer thing woke her up, but she figured her mother's response would probably have been the same either way. Karen stopped ten feet from her mother's door and looked around the hall. There were only a few pictures, all of them Mase in various military situations. One of her getting out of her jet, one receiving a medal, another jogging with a large flag on a pole. It looked more like the reception area of a recruiting office then a family home. There used to be a picture of Karen and her parents at a park, kicking a ball around, but Mase decided that it was "thematically dissimilar" and ought to be in another part of the house.

The other part of the house ended up being a kitchen drawer, underneath several of Mase's "lesser" awards.

"Karen Ernest Keller! You can get your ass in this room, or get the fuck out, but you will not homestead outside of my quarters huffing and puffing. Is that understood?"

Karen never really understood, but she went in anyway.

14. Normal being relative

Karen was trapped in that grim purgatory between being scared-to-death and bored-to-death. The view outside the cockpit never changed—just an unbroken, blue tunnel with no discernible form, yet totally consistent somehow. There were no sounds either. Well, almost no sounds. Karen could hear her back teeth grinding in the rhythm of "twinkle, twinkle, little star." She had first tried to count the passing time by marking down the amount of times she sang that eight second refrain, but she dropped the pencil under her seat, and the ship wouldn't allow her harness to unbuckle so she could get it.

By the time she'd finished calling the ship a motherfucker, she'd forgot how many marks she'd made on the page, then shortly afterward, forgot the song she was singing. All that was left over was the grinding. At some point, she'd tried to sleep, but couldn't. Or maybe she had. She didn't remember. The thing that bothered her at present was that she didn't feel like she was moving. She knew she was—well she *thought* she was, but it didn't feel right. No sense of gravity, no vibration, no acceleration or deceleration, just floating. Even floating wasn't quite right, because she missed the rising feeling that came with weightlessness.

The grinding picked up speed. It became less "twinkle, twinkle" and more "twinkletwinkletwinkletwi—"

MAJOR KELLER, how are you feeling? Your biometric readings have changed sharply."

"Fine! I'm, uh, I'm fine, there...spaceship."

Are you sure? Your heart rate suggests anxiety.

"Yeah, no, I'm just—nervous? I guess. It's hard to explain." It was hard for her to explain, because she couldn't put a label on exactly how she felt. Like everything since she'd entered the anomaly, her exact feelings became, well, indeterminable. Her thoughts bounced around, feeling like they were going to settle on one particular thing or another, then sort of blithely drift away to hover around something else.

Single-frame images of her mother, then her father, three or four bars from a song rolled into a possibly misremembered scene from a movie with members of the cast transposed from another.

For a moment, she thought she saw the cockpit window tremble, ever-so-slightly. She reached a gloved hand to touch the polyglass, but it was just beyond her reach, and would remain so. The ship would not allow the seat restraint to be released until the ship was safely down in whatever place lay beyond Bravo 42.

"So, uh, spaceship?" she asked, desperate to have an anchor point.

What can I do for you, MAJOR KELLER?

"Uh, shit" she hadn't thought of anything past "spaceship." She thought she saw the glass tremble again. "I— did you notice anything going on outside?"

The exterior optical arrays are non-functional. Secondary exterior sensors are intermittently functional.

"So, no then."

Affirmative.

"What is functional?"

Interior optical arrays, audio recorder, and life support are functioning normally.

"Ergh." Karen was teetering on the precipice of sulking, when an idea punched its way through trans-dimensional miasma and debilitating amphetamine come-down. "Hey, are the recorders active?"

Affirmative.

"How long have they been on?"

Recorders have been active since t-minus two hours until launch.

"And they're completely internal, right? Independent of the exterior arrays?"

Affirmative.

"Spaceship!" her shout fogged the inside of her visor. "What is the elapsed time on the recording as of right now?"

The elapsed time of the current recording is ten-thousand, five-hundred and twenty-six years, seven moths, seven days, fourteen hours, fifteen minutes. Would you like a rolling count of the seconds?

If there was anything in Karen's stomach, it would have washed the fog off of her visor. She thought her heart might explode. Every half remembered lesson and briefing about relativity and time-dilation came barreling through her head, like a gaggle of half-bright children shouting nonsense and leaving muddy footprints on the inside of her brain.

MAJOR KELLER, you s—

"Shut the fuck up! I don't want to hear about my motherfucking heart rate, you, you – ah, fuck! Of course my heart-rate's up! You just told me I've been stuck here for—uh, how long?"

The elapsed time of the current recording is two minutes and twenty, twenty one, tw-

"Shut up. The current recording, like after you said a million years, or whatever?"

The current recording has been active since t-minus two hours before launch.

"The recording that started two hours before launch has been recording for less than three minutes?"

Affirmative.

"Spaceship, are the interior recorders functioning normally?"

Affirmative.

Have you ever heard a molar crack? It's much worse in a sealed pilot's helmet.

15. The Only Question Worth Asking

Mase's bedroom wasn't as much a room as an aerospace museum with a custom princess bed, made by a bedraggled husband who wanted nothing more than for his suffering wife to be comfortable while he knitted tiny sweaters for cats. The inside of the room gave the impression that the photos and commendations on the hallway walls leading to the bedroom were unwanted guests being held at bay by a spectral accomplishments bouncer, determined to only let the most fabulous mementos inside.

A mosaic of printed and framed newsscans flanked either side of the wall behind the bed. Painstakingly detailed models of aircraft rested on wall-mounted shelves throughout the room, the most prominent of which being an exact replica of Mase's ZDD Danvers spacecraft, complete with a tiny, plastic figure of Mase sitting inside.

There was also a hideous floral-print chair in the corner of the room for "guests." That's where Karen sat.

Mase sat at the edge of the bed, legs crossed, her creeping dementia seemingly not affecting her military posture. She stared at the ceiling looking like she was on the ass-end of a conversation with the ionosphere.

"What do you want?"

"I got this notice," Karen crumpled the paper into a ball and threw it on Mase's lap. "Some army bullshit. Dad said it probably has something to do with you."

Mase unfurled the paper, smoothing it on her thigh. She had yet to actually look at Karen, but that wasn't atypical before her condition, and was standard operating procedure. She brought the paper close to her face, held it there for a moment, then took it back to her knee for more smoothing. Then back to her face, then to the knee. A deep breath then,

"Will you stop doing that and just read the goddamned thing already? It's as flat is it's gonna get!"

"Where did you get this?"

"Oh, I made it in a continuing education arts class. Happy Mother's Day!"

Karen's sarcasm was apparently powerful enough to break Mase's communication with her home planet, and she leveled her gaze at her daughter.

"Where did you get this, Karen?"

"Some army guy, I guess. He was wearing a uniform. Lots of buttons and pins and shit."

Mase looked back at the notice, then at Karen.

"Marine Corps."

"Whatever."

"No, not 'whatever', Karen. This notice is from the United States Marine Corps. Not the motherfucking Army. Perhaps if you did something a bit more ambitious than smoking marijuana with your father and failing to learn to play the trombone, like, oh I don't know, followed the news like an adult; you would know that the Army ceased to function several years ago. This piece of paper—I can't believe they'd waste such a valuable commodity on you—is an induction into the Marine Corps. I've tolerated your flippant attitude towards me and the life I've provided you, but you will respect the Corps. Is that understood?"

"Yes" Karen said, though the words coming through her clenched teeth sounded more like "yesshhhh."

"Good. So why are you here?"

"Dad said you might know what it was."

"Well, I've answered. Also, it's fairly clear by the simplistic language used in the document what its intent is" Mase casually backhanded the notice from her lap, to the floor, and resumed her ceiling-staring. "So," she continued, "I suppose the question is: why are you still here?"

Karen stood up, trying to glower at her mother, but in effect, just angrily staring at her collarbone. "So, that's it, huh? No greeting, no concerns, no questions?"

"I asked you several questions. You've failed to answer the most recent."

"What? Why I'm still here?"

Mase laid all the way down, back flat against the mattress. Her head never moved.

"I'm glad that I was able to furnish a life for you, and most likely, be so exemplary at my profession that it looks that you may be able to ride my coattails to a fulfilling career. You can go now, Karen."

"Yeah? Well...fuck you, you psycho!"

"Why are you st—" Karen slammed the door so hard that it startled her father, causing him to drop his bong onto the unforgiving kitchen tile; shattering it into several unglueable pieces.

Really, it was a tough day for everyone.

16. Before I Refuse to Answer your Questions, I have a Statement to Make

Karen's helmet had teeny-tiny vacuums built in just on either side of her jaw; which was helpful when she spat the blood from her broken tooth out, but less so when half of said broken tooth got stuck in one of the intake screens and made a noise like a fat guy attacking a milkshake for several dozen minutes, until Karen finally convinced the computer to shut it off.

Again, MAJOR, I must advise against disabling the upper fluid-extraction system. The vacuums are in place to prevent a mission-catastrophic event, such as asphyxiation due to vomit, excessive phl—

"Are you going to unlock the helmet, so I can get get the fucking tooth out of the thing?"

MAJOR, as I have previously made you aware, the PLS seal cannot be breached prior to arrival.

"Whelp, I guess we're going to have to roll the dice on my not drowning in my own puke" she said, taking a quick glance to confirm nothing outside had changed. It hadn't. "Which, by the way, ick. Has that happened before?"

```
    Pilots'   records   are   sealed   at   your
clearance level.
```

"Awesome. So, what can we talk about? I'm boooored."

```
    I'm  sorry MAJOR.  I  lack  the  capacity  for
dynamic  individual  conversation.  I  can  only
answer  queries  and  suggest  actions  as
appropriate.
```

"How do you know what's appropriate?"

```
    Natural  Language  Understanding  Processor
and  Semantic  Parsers  pathway  determiners  are
sealed at your clearance level.
```

"So, I have a high enough clearance to fly a secret mission to another dimension, but I don't have enough stroke to be allowed to know how a computer works?"

```
    Affirmative.
```

Karen banging her helmet into the headrest prompted the computer to inform her that repeated cranial impact could be avoided by second-level mobility reduction. Not wanting to find out what that was in word or action, Karen resolved to continue her physical protest with less showy techniques like breaking teeth and chewing holes into the inside of her face. Carefully, she tilted her head to the right, to look out into the anomaly.

There was no difference, just the same tunnel of textured blue that she started to fear would literally never end. She'd be trapped in this seat, unstuck in time, being informed that she didn't have the Government's permission to turn on the radio. For eternity.

She didn't even notice any of the slight tremors that had caught her eye earlier, but at that point she chalked those up completely to drug related quirks. As soon as the word "drugs" danced across her cortex, she wished she had some weed. She thought of her father. She *knew* he had weed. She should have asked him to hide some in her luggage. No one on base had any, or liked her enough to tell her they did. She wondered if her father was thinking about her.

The Marines hadn't allowed calls or visits, fearing it would distract her from the mission. How she could be distracted from being strapped into a rocket that didn't need her guidance and fired off somewhere that she couldn't navigate to, she couldn't guess. She figured he thought about her, but for all she knew, he'd been dead a hundred years already. Her heart sank. She didn't have a ton of friends, and none that anyone would consider close. It was just her, Ernie, and

"Hey, spaceship."

Yes, MAJOR?

"You, uh, worked with—for? For, I guess, my mother. Right?"

    I was CAPTAIN MASON-KELLER'S conveyance for all of her off-world flights.

"Well, then" Karen said, instantly regretting it, "tell me about her."

    Affirmative, MAJOR: I'll tell you about your mother.

Her jaw clenched, and she immediately remembered why she shouldn't do that. She made a command decision to chew on her tongue while the computer blathered.

    Mason, Katherine Louise. Captain, United States Marine Corps, Aircraft Group Eleven. Nigerian. Age forty-six. Born in Lagos on 15 March, 2061; naturalized after induction into the Marine Corps. Flew seventeen combat sorties in REDACTED. Awarded Navy Cross in REDACTED for REDACTED. Awarded Distinguished Flying Cross in REDACTED for REDACTED. Honorably Discharged 2 February 2085. Married Keller, Ernest Jerome of Cleveland, Ohio on 22 September, 2086. Gave birth to Keller, Karen Ernest on 25 December, 2086. Recalled to service on REDACTED for REDACTED. Returned from REDACTED on REDACTED. Filed report on MISSING to—

"Pause."

Record has been paused, MAJOR.

"Replay that from the part about being recalled."

Recalled to service on REDACTED for REDACTED. Returned from REDACTED on REDACTED. Filed report on MISSING t—

"Pause!"

Record is paused.

"What does 'report on missing' mean, exactly? The report is on something that's missing? Someone?"

The report, and all contextual information regarding that report are unavailable.

"Why?"

Unavailable.

"The report's unavailable? Or the explanation?"

Unavailable.

"So, it was redacted too."

Negative.

"If it wasn't redacted, then what happened? Did it get lost?"

Un—

"Don't you fucking say 'unavailable' to me again!"

The report does not exist.

It didn't seem that her tongue was going to finish the trip intact, either. If things kept going the way they were, she was going to have to figure out how to chew on her uvula.

17. Daughter, Be of Good Comfort

Ernie didn't talk the whole time he was loading Karen's luggage into the back of his truck. He knew the look on her face, he'd seen it on his own enough times. The look of a person that'd just been beaten down by the heavy cudgels that were his wife's insults.

He'd also recently downloaded an application to his media device that taught him a new word every time he went to watch a movie.

They drove a dozen miles or so toward Corvallis before he spoke up. "You alright, Bug? You're looking a bit woebegone."

"What?"

"Disconsolate?"

Karen squinted one eye and stared at him. "Dad, I don't know what the fuck you're talking about."

"I just mean that you look sad. No need to be so laconic."

"Are you going to talk like that the whole trip?"

"Sorry, Bug. Just trying to better myself a little, you know?"

"You're fine the way you are."

"Ah, everyone could stand to improve on something, Kar."

Karen rolled her eyes and turned to stare out the window. In any other situation, she'd be happy to be in the truck. Ernie owned it since she could remember, and any time they would do things together, the truck would be involved. That half of the time 'doing things together' involved *working* on the truck was immaterial. Ernie loved that truck. He told Karen once that he loved fixing up old, broken things. Karen figured that explained the deal with her

"—other."

"Huh?"

"Your mother. What did you say to her?"

Karen sighed and threw her head into her seat's headrest. "Nothing, really. I showed her the notice, and she thanked me for riding her coattails. Then she told me to leave."

"That's it?"

"Well, she thinks you should stop smoking so much weed. And she brought up my great trombone disgrace."

"She mentioned that again, huh?" Ernie laughed.

"Well, it's only been twelve years. These things take time to get over."

Ernie laughed again, and lit a cigarette. They were increasingly hard to come by, and he could really only get away with smoking them in the truck. It was old, and smelled weird; and smoking cigarettes was de facto banned by public opinion just about everywhere. He knew Karen didn't particularly care for them either, but she rarely said anything.

"Bug, you gotta give your mom a break."

"Nope."

"No, I mean it. She tries, y'know? It's just that—like the trombone, right? I think she brings it up so much, because she's—"

"A control-freak maniac that's never been bad at anything?"

"Well yeah, I guess, partially. But, more than that, it's just—she doesn't really know you. Not really."

"Is that supposed to make me feel better?"

"Yeah. I guess, I mean—" Ernie had a hard time putting the words together. Mase and Karen's relationship had always been dicey, but since Mase became housebound, it morphed into flat-out volatile.

"So, the only time your mom's really been around, besides now, was when you were little, right?"

"Yeah, so?"

"So, right before she got called back into the service was when you were so excited about the trombone. You showing an intr—hang on."

Ernie scratched his tongue with his index finger, looked at the cigarette filter for a second, then flicked it out the window. "Sorry. Anyway, because you were so excited about it, she was too. All she talked about was the goddamned trombone. And about how you could get a scholarship, what was the right size for you, where should we go, real or synthbrass—you get the idea."

"Still not really seeing the point."

"Well, shut up a second and let me finish."

He reached for the pack of cigarettes in the console, shook it, then threw it out the window.

"She got so wound up about that goddamned thing, and you played it for what? Two weeks before you shitcanned it?"

"I was twelve."

"Right, I know. But don't forget, your mom left shortly after, and you guys weren't really around each other—well, not much, until the last year or so. The trombone thing is one of the only really vivid memories she has of you. Like, when you weren't a baby, I mean."

"Uh, okay. I still don't feel any better."

"I guess you wouldn't. But, really, it doesn't matter," Ernie said, trying to keep the shaky steering wheel straight with his right hand, while digging between the seat and door with his left, "Maybe Kath isn't the best mother. But she's great at being Katherine. Just like you're great at being you. She can't be you any better than you can, so don't worry too much about what she thinks."

Ernie's left hand shot into the air, a slightly bent cigarette between his index finger and thumb like a talisman.

"I'm not really sure what being me actually entails."

Ernie lit the cigarette and took a deep pull.

"Bug, I get the feeling that you're going to find out pretty soon."

18. Day Destroys the Night

Keller: —s is on, right? I thought there'd be an icon on the HUD. **[pause]** Are you sure it's on? **[pause]** Huh? **[pause]** The microphone icon, yeah I see it. **[pause]** I don't know what Cheyenne means. **[pause]** I don't know what cyan is either. **[pause]** Well, why didn't you just say that? **[pause]** I don't know, spaceship! I didn't go to fucking art school! **[undetermined clicking sound]** Fine, I'll leave it on. **[pause]** No, it's fine. **[pause]** Because I don't *feel* like getting the portable recorder and rebreather. Can I just do this? Please? **[pause]** Yes, I will alert you if I need assistance. Christ almighty.

[at this point there are two minutes and twenty seven seconds of what have are believed to be sounds indicating ambulation]

Keller: Uh, okay. This is the initial report from Karen-uh, Major Keller. Karen. Major Karen Keller, reporting from the area beyond the Bravo 42 anomaly. I exited the anomaly at, well, it felt like a few minutes ago, but none of the instruments really work right, so I'm not sure. But I'd bet recently. Fairly. Am I shouting? I feel like I'm shouting. **[pause]** I guess. I just feel shouty, y'know? So, as best as I can describe it, we didn't really set down on anything so much as a landing area sort of appeared underneath the ship. I asked the ship if it was like the other trips that it'd made, but apparently I'm not important enough to know that, which is helpful; so thanks for the shitty clearance.

The landing area, well, the thing is, it was grey; like pavement kinda, but as I've been standing here, a lot of it seems to have turned green. It sort of looks like grass now. **[pause]** Scratch that, it looks exactly like grass. I'd examine it further, but the ship won't unlock the glove cuffs on my suit. **[pause]** I know that! I'm telling *them*. Anyway, so somehow the ground around me went from grey asphalt-ish to green grass in a matter of minutes. Or maybe it always was grass, and the grey was some optical illusion, or like a weird refraction thing. Standby, I'll see if I can replay the video from my helmet optics.

[the audio feed stops for four minutes and nineteen seconds]

Keller: So, this is probably going to sound weird, but my personal video log is somehow a two minute video of a kitten playing in a shoe, on a loop. Look, I don't know if there's something wrong with the ship, which to be honest, has been acting especially weird since we got to the anomaly; or if it's tied somehow to whatever this—*place* is. **[pause]** Well, you have. **[pause]** Yes, you have. **[pause]** Well, what if I need to take the fucking glove off for some task that requires dexterity beyond a big, clunky, space-mitten? **[pause]** I fucking heard you about the protocols! Why do you get to decide that?

[audio feed stops for one minute and thirty-eight seconds]

Keller: Once again, I have to commend you all for sending me out here with a clearance level that's not sufficient to take a shit, without the ship running a risk-analysis. Back to the log: there appears to be some kind of atmosphere, as I can see the grass blowing around a little, but I can't confirm that via sensors. The topography seems similar, if not identical to earth, I mean, at least where I'm standing right now. In the distance, maybe a couple of miles—shit, am I supposed to report in kilometers? Doesn't matter, 'cause I can't really estimate either very well. At any rate, it looks like there's hills? Or are they buildings? I thought they were—Well, there's something...*vertical* in the distance. I think I'm gonna go—hang on. It looks like—is that? That's a person? Stand by.

[transmission ends]

19. No mistakes, just happy accidents

Ernie and Karen didn't talk a whole lot during the drive from Telluride to Corvallis. They made noise, for sure; singing songs, quoting movies back and forth at each other, and played an interminable game of *I Spy* that mostly consisted of cow and barn related items. They also complained at length about the Colorado Rockies off-season; most of the venom directed toward the signing of Troy Tulowitzki the fourth, a .236 lifetime hitter with no pop and a wet noodle for an arm that only got a contract because of his name. The noise filled the air, and the air filled the time, but not much of either was substantial.

He wanted to tell her that he was worried about her, but he didn't want to worry *her*. Military action hadn't been favorable to any of the Kellers. Besides the issues with Mase, Ernie's father and one of his sisters had been killed in the service. His father was the victim of an improvised explosive on the St-Bernard-de-Lacolle in Quebec during the secession spillover; his sister a more spectacular one, gunned down on a successful raid during the Battle of Dallas. Ernie, not wanting to kill anyone, nor particularly interested in getting killed, abstained from service; although marrying Mase, he never really escaped it entirely.

Somewhere in Lincoln County, Idaho, he realized he was chain-smoking. In rhythm, he'd smoke down to about half an inch before the filter, flick it out of the window, take a sip of whatever beverage he had at the time, then light another. Once he realized, he took a break from the smokes, and stole a glance at his daughter, who'd nodded off in the passenger seat, drooling on her sweatshirt. He was astounded at how much she really looked like her mother, although with a softer face, a trait most likely inherited from him; the Kellers always tended toward stoutness.

He didn't know his wife's family. To be fair, she didn't really know them either, she was raised by an aunt after her parents were rounded up by Nigerian troops with the rest of the "dissidents." Mase didn't know anything about her parents' political activities, just that her mother was an architect and her father was a schoolteacher. Mase's aunt had told her that her parents were "too smart for their own damned good," and to "let that be an example to you." Ernie wasn't surprised to learn that his wife left Lagos at her earliest possible moment, escaping to the waiting arms of the United States Military.

Ernie's family, on the other hand, was close as could be, even after part of it was exploded and part was perforated. They gathered often to watch sports, crack jokes, have meals, and a multitude of other activities that made his wife visibly uncomfortable when she came with him to visit; before they walled themselves up in Colorado. When she did visit with him, she seemed to spend a lot of time jogging. Like for four or five hours a day. Her in-laws always tried to feed her or include her, and while Mase was polite, she never seemed to warm up to them.

Ernie overheard Mase ask his mother once, "Is everyone always this—affectionate?" When his mother answered in the affirmative, Mase simply said: "Hmm."

But, that was his wife, and he loved her. Even if she was aloof and weird. And she loved him. And, unlike a lot of people, he could say that he knew as a matter of absolute fact, because she recorded damned near everything about her day-to-day life. He'd see text displays on her computer that he learned were transcripts of some kind of thought-log she kept, and in many of them, there'd be touching things she thought about Ernie, things she'd never really say, but apparently thought about a lot. He didn't feel bad about reading them, well, not too bad, because she would just leave them open on whatever device she used.

Obfuscation was not something that was a part of his wife's makeup, unless it had something to do specifically with her work. Even then, knowing her, if someone plainly asked her a question about it, she'd probably answer it. Most likely, if Ernie didn't know something, it was because Ernie didn't ask. Ernie, partially to protect her, and mostly because he genuinely didn't want to know, didn't ask a whole lot. Mase would certainly talk to him, before the incident, anyway; she just wasn't, well, dynamic when it came to conversation.

"Mmmph, take it easy with the smokes, Dad. Sstinks in here."

"Yeah, okay. Sorry, Bug," he said, just realizing he hadn't really stopped smoking when he thought he did. "How're you feeling?"

"Sssleepy. Huuungry. My neck hurts."

"You want me to pull over?"

"Maybe. Later. I dunno."

"Something on your mind, kiddo?"

"Had a nightmare."

"What about?"

"Mom. The hospital."

"Oh." That wasn't new. Karen had been having a version of the same nightmare since the MPs brought Mase home. The gist of it was Karen trying to pull Mase's arm away, but not being able to, as Mase set fire to the hospital.

"Why'd she do it?"

"Oh, Karen. Your mom, she's sick, y'know? Who knows why?"

"Why do you think she did it?"

Ernie lit a cigarette, not noticing he already had one in his mouth. He flicked out the old one and started on the new.

"Honestly? I think she thought she was protecting them."

"Why in the fuck would you *think* that?"

Ernie sighed. He tightened his hands on the steering wheel to camouflage their trembling. "Something she said.

When they brought her home, she looked at me, totally stone-faced and said 'They don't know what I know. If they knew what was coming, they'd understand.'"

"Huh. I figured it was just because she hates kids."

"Your mother doesn't hate kids."

"Coulda fooled me" she paused to adjust the neck on her sweatshirt. "Seriously, why'd she want to have me anyway?"

Ernie scrambled to think of something to say. He landed on "Well—" and nothing else.

"I should've guessed. I was a fucking accident" Karen said, crossing her arms. She opened her mouth to say something else, thought better of it, and shook her head; it came to a stop parallel to her right shoulder, so she could stare out the window. Ernie, not knowing what would make her feel better, settled on stumbling through the truth.

"Well, no, not—your mother and I, well, me mostly, we—I...yes, Bug you were an accident. But, so what? Lots of things are accidents, doesn't make 'em bad; doesn't mean they shouldn't have happened. Doesn't mean we didn't need them. Velcro, X-Rays, fucking microwaves – shit the Universe, probably. All just big accidents, but most things are, really. That's life, Kar—just people bouncing around the world, making shit happen, whether they meant to or not.

Shit, if your mother hadn't sprained her ankle, she'd never have been home for us to, uh, make you. You know what? I'm glad she sprained her ankle. In fact, I'd cut her *and* my feet off just to make sure you came around. Don't get so hung up on plans and order. The last time I followed a plan, I burned a cake and ruined the oven. Y'know what I mean, jellybean?"

Karen looked at Ernie and half-smiled. "So I turned out better than the cake?"

"Hey, let's not go crazy."

20. A Bit More Substantial than "Wash Me"

Karen Keller was a woman that feared a lot of things: her mother, public restrooms, the phone ringing, crickets; you know, the usual. Weirdly, landing in another dimension and walking toward a vague figure as it closed on her in kind didn't make the cut.

"Do you see that? Can you tell if it's a person?"

MAJOR KELLER, your helmet's optical arrays are still non-functional.

"So, that's a 'no,' huh? No radar or whatever either?"

All exterior arrays on the craft and the PLS suit are non-functional, with the exception of the audio recorders.

"Great, so if it eats me, they'll be able to hear me crunch and scream."

Assuming your equipment can be recovered, affirmative.

"God, we can only hope" she said, continuing her brisk stride.

The area surrounding her was a thick fog that was mostly opaque, but she found that if she stopped to stare, it seemed to become transparent, and she could make out the ground. She didn't particularly feel like focusing on the ground, though. She wanted to see what this thing was walking toward her. The shape seemed human, but not enough that she'd swear to it. Besides, why shouldn't it be human-shaped? She half-remembered one of the Lab Weirdos babbling about soap bubbles and optimal people-shapes, but his voice was so nasally that she checked out before the third time he said "carbon."

It took her a second to notice she'd stopped walking in order to recall the bubble-talk. Then she realized that the figure had stopped too. She waited for it to move. It didn't. Karen took a tentative step toward it. The figure did the same. Karen took a second step; the figure mirrored her.

MAJOR KELLER, is everything alright? Your heart rate ha—

"Yeah, shut the fuck up a minute" she whispered. She could feel her pulse quicken, without a robot blabbing in her ear; but still she wasn't afraid. She felt like she should be afraid that she wasn't afraid, but no dice. She felt—hopeful? She couldn't place the feeling, but it was good. She thought maybe it was some kind of Astronaut-specific feeling. Cosmo—no. Astro...vescent? She liked astrovescent. "Spaceship, remember 'astrovescent."

Context needed.

"Ugh, just remember the word, it's like, space-happy" she said, still looking at the unmoving figure."

Noted. Astro-vescent: possible portmanteau of astronaut and effervescent.

"Yeah, thanks" Karen said. Positively overcome by the emotion she just invented, she did the goofiest thing she could think of.

She started skipping.

The figure matched her bounce. Mid skip, she waved. It waved too; that made her skip faster. She wondered if the gravity wherever here was, was the same as on Earth. After it occurred to her, she thought she was a little higher in the air, but she couldn't be sure. With each bounce, the distance between her and the figure drew narrower. She didn't notice her surroundings at all any more. She didn't care. She just needed to see whatever this was, up close. Her need to see became rapturous.

She stopped skipping, and started sprinting. The figure matched her stride-for-stride. She couldn't tell how far apart they were, but she knew they were getting close. She was glad the suit was slimmer than all the ones in the old photos, as it allowed her to run comfortably. Her breath grew heavy. She ignored it. The computer kept trying to get her attention. She shut it out. Nothing mattered, nothing but the figure. Not far now.

She could make out some of the finer details of the figure: it was definitely bi-pedal, two arms, normal amount of heads, definitely, distinctly human. Maybe six feet tall? Even if her helmet optics and sensors were working, her head was bobbling too violently to get an accurate reading. The figure wasn't particularly large, nor small. She thought it might be a male, but couldn't tell.

She would soon; just a few hundred feet seemed to separate them. She sucked in one huge breath and shifted into a gear she didn't know she had. The weight of the helmet forced her head down. The heavy thud of her boots on the ground rattled all the way up to her broken tooth. She spit blood onto the inside of her visor. She wouldn't be stopped.

And because she wouldn't be stopped, she slammed headfirst into the figure's chest. Karen felt a searing pain in her neck, but as soon as she realized it was there, it went away. She looked up, ready to see what the thing was, ready to record every minute detail of its appearance, like she'd been trained to.

But she couldn't. Not because she wasn't capable, but because it wasn't possible, not in any meaningful way. The figure appeared to be a male human, who looked familiar to her, but she couldn't place the face. He had a dark complexion, then a medium, then fair, then kind of all of them at once. His irises seemed to change every time it blinked. It smiled at Karen.

"Wh-who are you?" she asked.

The figure leaned toward her with its mouth open. After a few seconds, her visor was completely fogged over. Before she had time to say anything, a large dot appeared at the top of the left side of her visor. The dot became a line. The line became this: A. It took up half of the visor.

Next to that, another dot formed. Then an arc. The arc became this: Ω.

MAJOR KELLER, are you

21. Fun with Acronyms

February 13, 2098
Release # 56412596-20
For Immediate Release to the Office of the Secretary of Defense

Madame Secretary,

What follows is a summary of the events of operation SPACE EAGLE, and the plan for the subsequent operation, tentatively, and heretofore referred to as operation CELESTIAL FIST. As with all documents regarding SPACE EAGLE, all communiques regarding CELESTIAL FIST are considered Clearance Code Ultra, and are for your eyes only.

<u>Space Eagle</u>

23, June 2097, 1422 hours: The ZDD-*Danvers* craft MASON-KELLER was piloting alerts the operations center at Lamoni that it has returned from the area beyond the Bravo 42 relay, although all telemetry from the ship and a satellite in proximity show no sign of the craft ever deviating from its flight path. Per SOP, the craft's leash beacon activates, and craft begins its return planeside at 1424.

23, June 2097, 1437 hours: Craft re-enters orbit. Ionization blackout prevents communication with the craft for twelve minutes.

23, June 2097, 1449 hours: Craft reports splashdown off the coast of Port Charlotte, FL. USMC helicopter confirms landing at 1452. Helicopter and Lamoni command center attempt to radio MASON-KELLER. No response.

23, June 2097, 1530 hours: USMC retrieval unit recovers craft, along with MASON-KELLER, who is alive, but unresponsive. Keller is couriered to a secure unit at Walter Reed NMMC. In Bethesda, MD The craft is shipped to the Clearance Ultra hangar at the Naval Air Station in Patuxent River, MD.

24, June 2097, 0830 hours: Doctors at Walter Reed report that MASON-KELLER is awake, and passed all cursory physical examinations. Report also states that MASON-KELLER seems disoriented and rambles, so a CT scan is ordered. A psychiatrist typically used in sensitive ops is also sent for.

24, June 2097, 1100 hours: Technicians at Patuxent River finish the evaluation of the craft. The technicians report no retrievable data that would suggest that the craft went anywhere beyond the recorded flight path, although they also report multiple inconsistencies between the recordings from the craft's on-board recorders, and the data they were able to retrieve from MASON-KELLER's PLS helmet. The PLS helmet and suit are sent to Lamoni.

24, June 2097, 1325 hours: The Walter Reed doctors receive MASON-KELLER's CT scan. There is a problem, but the cleared doctors don't have the expertise to report thoroughly on it. A request is sent to Joint Special Operations Command [JSOC] to request temporary clearance for a neurologist from Johns

Hopkins. While the request is pending, the psychiatrist examines MASON-KELLER.

24, June 2097, 1530 hours: The psychiatrist's evaluation is inconclusive. The report states that MASON-KELLER is aloof, but confused. At several points during the interview, he reports that she begins to talk, stops, then stares out the window. After thirty minutes of questioning, he states that MASON-KELLER refused to answer at all. Psychiatrist suggests that she could "simply be overwhelmed," or could have suffered some kind of trauma. The psychiatrist requests a re-interview for a week later, which is approved by the CMO at Walter Reed.

25, June 2097, 0600 hours: MASON-KELLER's PLS gear arrives at Lamoni. Technicians state that the will have all the data downloaded and collated by 0800.

25, June 2097, 0630 hours: JSOC approves the request to have the Neurologist review MASON-KELLER's CT scan, but will not issue clearance. JSOC suggests to Walter Reed to present the CT scan to the Neurologist as part of a blind case study.

25, June 2097, 0758 hours: The Lamoni technicians submit their initial report. According to the PLS system, the time elapsed on MASON-KELLER's flight was thirty-three years. The helmet's optical arrays failed to record anything from launch to splashdown. The technicians' attempt to verbally interface with the PLS was unsuccessful. The PLS told the technicians that they were not at a sufficient clearance level to receive trip-data beyond the time-elapsed. The technicians' request more time to examine the helmet and suit, which is approved by MORRISON, LAURA, COL.

25, June 2097, 1245 hours: After reviewing MASON-KELLER's CT scan, the Hopkins neurologist concludes the following:

MASON-KELLER's brain has several occurrences of White-Matter Hyperintensities [WMHs] consistent with the brain of a person that has suffered micro-hemorrhages in the brain, typically over the age of sixty. As of this writing, MASON-KELLER is thirty-six years old. Neurologist states that WHMs can cause cognitive impairments. Neurologist requests previous scans form patient, request is forwarded to JSOC.

25, June 2097, 1255 hours: Request for prior CT scans denied by JSOC.

25, June 2097, 1638 hours: Second report from Lamoni technicians filed. The PLS helmet diagnostic shows several hundred thousand neural-link downloads from MASON-KELLER. The data received from the downloads in encrypted in a manner a-typical of USMCNASA protocols. The PLS continues refuses to respond verbally to anyone except for MASON-KELLER. A request to transfer MASON-KELLER to Lamoni is initiated by MORRISON. Technicians also find what appear to be soil samples on MASON-KELLER's boots and gloves, but are unequipped to analyze them. The samples are sent to the Marine Corps Warfighting Laboratory in Quantico, VA.

26, June 2097, 0700 hours: JSOC approves MASON-KELLER's transfer, with the proviso that the Walter Reed psychiatrist examines her within five days. MORRISON will arrange the travel for the psychiatrist to the Lamoni facility. The objection to the transfer from BANNER, JOSHUA- CMO is noted at 26 June, at 0900.

27, June 2097, 1030 hours: MASON-KELLER arrives at Lamoni. The flight technicians, who report her to be evasive and "odd", interview her. A call is made to have MORRISON assist with the interview. MORRISON is en route as of 1100 hours

27, June 2097, 1142 hours: The Marine Warfighting Laboratory files the sample data report. The results are unquantifiable. The samples are wholly molecularly dissimilar from any matter recorded from our Solar System. The report suggests that the matter is possibly from somewhere in deep space, but have no point of reference. The Laboratory will re-test samples.

27 June 2097, 1720 hours: MORRISON arrives to debrief MASON-KELLER. When MASON-KELLER becomes belligerent, MORRISION orders MASON-KELLER to assist the technicians. When MASON-KELLER vocalizes, the PLS becomes cooperative. MASON-KELLER instructs the PLS to tell the technicians "what they want to know."

28, June 2097, 0530 hours: The Warfighting Laboratory files the re-test reports. They are identical to the first. The Laboratory reports the margin of error to be less than one-tenth of a percent.

28, June 2097, 0811 hours: The PLS debriefing is delayed due to the death of one of the technicians. RAGOLIA, NATHAN, SPEC. was found in his quarters, dead from exsanguination, possibly due to self-inflicted wounds. Military Police are investigating the incident. PLS debriefing to be resumed TBA, with the arrival of a cleared technician from the Joint Reserve Base at Fort Worth.

29, June 2097, 1151 hours: The psychiatrist arrives in a transport, along with the technician to Fort Worth. The psychiatrist begins the re-interview with MASON-KELLER at 1227 hours. MORRISON observes. The objection to MORRISON's observation by LARKIN, MICHAEL M.D. is noted on 29 June at 1228 hours.

29, June 2097, 1335 hours: The tech team discovers an audio log recorded by the PLS helmet at an interminable point, while ostensibly in the area beyond the Bravo 42 anomaly. The recording indicates a voice beside that of MASON-KELLER. The voice appears to say "Katherine, go home." The PLS cannot identify the voice. Waveform analysis is inconsistent with human vocal patterns.

29, June 2097, 1500 hours: LARKIN completes interview with MASON-KELLER. He determines that MASON-KELLER is unfit to continue service. LARKIN will file a full report after returning to Walter Reed. MORRISON submits the audio log from the interview room.

30, June 2097, 0700 hours: The PLS is no longer cooperative, insisting that it will not furnish any further information without MASON-KELLER present. A request is made to have MASON-KELLER return to the hangar. MORRISON denies the request. MASON-KELLER is ordered to write a complete mission debriefing.

1, July 2097, 0800 hours: LARKIN's report is submitted. The report is unable to be reproduced, due to data corruption.

2, July 2097, 1100 hours: MASON-KELLER's debriefing is filed. The debriefing is classified CODE: BLACK by JSOC. MASON-KELLER is discharged and returned home to Colorado. MASON-KELLER's PLS is locked in a secure unit in Lamoni, and the craft is grounded pending further instructions.

14, July 2097 through 2, September 2097: MOORE, DOUGLAS, CAPT.; STAMBAUGH, ANDREW, LT.; DUELLA, STANLEY MAJ. Each fly missions to the Bravo 42 anomaly. All three are KIA via soluble discorporation. All craft are undamaged and contain no useful data.

3, September 2097: MASON-KELLER is recalled to USMCNASA.

5, September 2097, 1820 hours: MASON-KELLER returns from the Bravo 42 anomaly, with her original PLS unit, and craft. Debriefing is CODE: BLACK pending JSOC release. MASON-KELLER is sent to Walter Reed for testing.

6, September 2097, 0600 hours: MASON-KELLER's CT scan reveals a twenty percent increase in white-matter hyperintensities. MASON-KELLER is classified 4-F by BANNER, JOSHUA.

10, September through 14, November 2097: MASON-KELLER completes five more trips to Bravo 42. Requests to send MASON-KELLER to Walter Reed for examination are denied by JSOC. MASON-KELLER's debriefings become increasingly erratic. MORRISON is able to convince MASON-KELLER to make the PLS cooperate with the technicians.

19, November 2097, 0800 hours: A scrubbed story regarding MASON-KELLER's flights is leaked to *The Washington Post* in an effort to retard what JSOC believes is a similar operation from the Chinese.

21, November 2097, 0630 hours: MASON-KELLER is discharged. A stipend is granted for her home care.

30, November 2097, 0415 hours: All of MASON-KELLER's reports are collated with the audio logs recorded by the PLS. The neural uploads, now numbering in the millions, are still encrypted, with a rotating cipher. Best technical estimate can expect the cipher to be decrypted in seventy years, with current technology. A plus-ninety percent accurate report is created from the available collated data. The report is sealed by JSOC, and a Clearance-level ultra summary is compiled for distribution to the Office of the Department of Defense.

Space Eagle Findings

The area beyond the Bravo 42 anomaly has been determined to exist in a physical, although unquantifiable space; occupied by at least one (1) Non-Human Entity [NHE]. Due to **[redacted]** communication with the NHE(s) is not achievable. It is the opinion of the USMC and JSOC that the Bravo 42 anomaly and space beyond is an existential threat to the United States and its interests. An operation to neutralize the situation is in the planning stages.

Addendum 28, December: All operations involving MASON-KELLER are unilaterally suspended due to the St. Marten's Children's Hospital incident. MASON-KELLER is to be considered under house arrest in perpetuity. A copy of her PLS is to be installed in her home and vehicles to monitor her movements and activities. A surviving child identified MASON-KELLER as the arsonist, recognizing her from television. A Crisis-Response Team extracted the boy, and placed him in a facility at the Lamoni site. The CRT has scrubbed all mentions of MASON-KELLER.

Celestial Fist

Per the findings of SPACE EAGLE, a plan has been devised to deliver ordnance sufficient to neutralize any threat posed by Bravo 42 or its inhabitants. The issue of soluble discorporation was solved, in part from an idea posed by MASON-KELLER's PLS. The PLS suggests that entry to Bravo 42 is determined at the genetic level, although the remaining technicians report that it cannot articulate how it arrived at that conclusion. With MASON-KELLER to participate, the PLS suggested that her daughter, KELLER, KAREN ERNEST may be able to enter Bravo 42. Follicle and dermal samples from KELLER were obtained during a routine medical exam. On 31, December, the samples were launched in MASON-KELLER's craft, to Bravo 42.

The craft was later retrieved, with the samples intact and unharmed. It was decided to go ahead with the operation using KELLER in her mother's PLS suit and Danvers craft in an effort to eliminate as many variables as possible. A draft notice was couriered to KELLER, while the craft was retrofitted with the ordnance. Due to the lack of training time and general questions regarding KELLER's reliability, JSOC insisted that the trip be completely automated, through the PLS. JSOC also ordered the neural up-link hardware removed from the PLS.

Obviously, we will update you further as the launch approaches.

Col. Laura Morrison,
Director, Special Project Corps
USMCNASA

22. Spectral Seating Logistics

On a scale from her grandmother's shed to the Air and Space museum, this fell closer to the latter on Karen's "List of weird places I've woken up."

Not the place, precisely, since she couldn't see much of it; more the circumstance, specifically being flat on her back, all of her extremities tingling like she'd managed to compress every nerve in her body simultaneously. She didn't have time to take good stock of her situation, as a pleasant-looking man-head filled her field of view.

"Hey buddy," said the man-head.

His voice came through her helmet, clear as day, but not through the speakers; more like in her thoughts than her ears. Not crazy-loud but the fidelity was incredible, not too different then when she'd recall how a great song sounded. She still wasn't scared, not quite, but she was anxious. The vibrations meandered up her fingers and toes to her forearms and shins. She tried to shake them out. They just moved further up.

"Uh, hi" Karen said. The man-head tilted and smiled, making Karen wonder if it could hear her. "Ah, shit. Spaceship, is the external speaker on?"

No, MAJOR. Is there a mission reason for which you'd like the speaker on?

"Well, yeah, obviously. I need to, er, communicate with whatever" she raised her arm toward the smiling face. At least she hoped she did. The vibrating made it difficult to tell if her limbs were actually responding.

MAJOR, the exterior arrays are still non-functional. I am aware of nothing beyond you.

"Aren't the audio—"

The man-head backed up a bit to reveal an entire, if not impressive body. It stretched their right arm out, waving faintly toward the sky. "Don't worry about the speakers, scooter. I can hear you fine."

Karen let out the tiniest yelp as her body stood upright, completely of its own accord. It felt like she was being pulled to her feet by a thousand invisible ropes—gentle, but awkward. She hung in place, totally transfixed by the man-thing that seemingly held her there. It cocked their head to the side again, its features scrunched up like a child concentrating.

"Oh, man—that's probably not too comfortable, right? Sorry, I don't host much. You probably want a chair, right? You guys still into chairs?"

"What?"

MAJOR are you in distress? Gyroscopic sensors indicate that you are standing at an—

Before the computer could continue, Karen's made a lobster-pinch gesture, rendering the helmet's speakers silent.

"Such a mother hen, right? I can't hear it, but I can tell by your face that it's clucking in your ear." he said, winking. "So, go ahead and cop a squat, the chair's right behind you."

Karen didn't get the chance to look behind her. The phantom strands holding her up relaxed, and she sank down into a much-too-cushy chair. But then, it wasn't too cushy. It seemed just...perfect. The area around was bright, dull, sharp, and foggy. The chair supplier stood across from her, beaming. Karen was confused.

"I'm confused."

He laughed. "It's a lot to process, right? Just take a deep breath, and relax. It'll come to you."

Karen tried to close her eyes, but the lids seemed to reverse polarity, snapping open as soon as they touched. She noticed that she was sitting in an office, brown wood paneling covered the walls. Through her boots, she could tell that there was a thick carpet beneath her. A dusty ceiling fan wobbled over a huge desk, behind which sat, sat—

"Wh... who are you, exactly?"

The body behind the desk shrugged. It was wearing a short-sleeved oxford shirt, with a novelty light-up tie spilling out from the collar. It's face still pleasant, underneath a shock of brown hair. Or blonde. Was it red? No it was definitely brown.

"You can take that helmet off, if you want."

"No thanks, I—who are you?"

"The Alpha and Omega thing not tip you off?"

"Alpha and Ohhh, shit. Am I fucking dead? I knew it. I knew this would happen."

A.O. plopped his bare feet on a stack of yellowing papers on the desk, and laughed. "You're not dead, buddy. Take it easy."

"How do I know I'm not dead?"

"You pick strange times to get philosophical."

Karen folded her arms across her chest, putting her boots on the desk in kind. She realized that the buzzing was no longer there. "I feel like I should be scared, or nervous, or— something. But I'm not. Why?"

A.O. rested its chin in their hands. "There's a fascinating biochemical explanation, that, knowing you like I do, you'd check out of in about thirty seconds. Ask me something else."

"How did you make the chair appear?"

"You penetrated time and space in a miracle of technological innovation, and your primary concern is chair logistics?"

"No, my *primary* concern was finding out who you are, which, I'm pretty sure you still haven't answered. How do you know my name?" Karen asked, trying to peer down to her flight suit, but it was obscured by the bottom of her helmet.

"Are you checking for a name tag?"

"N-no, of course—fucking who are you, already?"

Alph hopped on the desk, sitting cross-legged just to the side of Karen's boot. "I think you already know."

"Are you, you're, um, God?" she asked, the very words making her feel kind of dipshit-y as the tumbled out of her mouth. "Or, like, what, Jehovah?"

"The name isn't terribly important" he said, turning his palms upward, with a half-smile.

"So what should I call you?"

"Like I said, it's not important; I'm kind of beyond labels. But, if it helps you, then just pick something."

"Um, how about...Walter?"

"What, really? Okay."

"Of course you're a man. That's just perfect."

"Well, no. What you see is just the product of your little chimp-head collating a lot of data that you're not really equipped to process. Man, you guys were a riot when you were chimps. Totally adorable"

"So you're a woman?"

"Karen, sweetheart, do you really think I would have a gender? Why would I need one? Anyway, let's not get hung up on this. You, my little pal, are only the second person to come here, so, congratulations!" he gave her a strong thumbs-up. "Unfortunately, you're not really supposed to be here."

"Oh. Soooo, are you gonna bring me back to life?"

"Karen, again, I assure you that you're not dead. This is an actual, physical place that you've traveled to!"

"Can I ask you something?"

"Of course. We don't really have a lot of time, though, so keep it peppy."

"Uh, ok" she said, dropping her feet down to the hard, tile floor. "So, only me and my mother have been here."

"That's not a question."

"Hey, man, bear with me. I didn't bring my deity interview script."

"Fair."

"Right. So, are we special? Is it like a prophecy? Everyone else melted."

So, in cosmic horror, it's fairly for a person to meet a creator that despises them. What's generally not covered, is when a person meets their creator and it laughs its ethereal balls off at them. To call this just a laugh, though, is to be an insufferable reductionist.

The sound that erupted from Walter was at least a guffaw, bordering on a flat-out roar that drastically changed the atmosphere in the room. Even though Karen had not thought she might be a child of destiny until literally seconds ago, she was still a little hurt that she wasn't.

"What? The laughing? Sorry, I don't get a lot of opportunities to converse, even less to laugh. Don't be grumpy, buddy, it's just that—never mind. To answer your question, though, you and Katherine are as special as every one of your species; which is to say, not very.”

“And that's funny?”

“Well, yeah.”

Karen stood up, turned on her heel, and walked toward the door. The door didn't cooperate. Every step she took pushed the far side of the room another ten feet away.

“Karen, where are you going?”

She kept walking, saying nothing. Her stride increased, but the end of the room moved exponentially farther away.

“Karen, you can't leave.”

“And yet, here I go.”

She picked up the pace further. Not only did the wall keep moving, but the floor inclined. She trudged onward, straining, barely moving forward, until the floor rose so sharply that she tumbled backwards, slamming into the desk. A smiling Walter looked down on her.

“Don't you still want to know why you're here?”

“I fell down the floor.”

"Yes, and that was *also* hysterical. But, since you're here, don't you really want to know how you're here when everyone else they sent can be exhumed with a straw?"

"I feel like you *really* want to tell me."

Karen wondered if the ship could hear her. She'd gotten used to its not-quite-human voice chirping in her ear. "It's your universe, apparently; so, y'know, 'do you."

"I do really want to tell you, actually. Like I said, I don't get guests often. So, have you ever heard someone say something like 'there's infinite possible combinations of genotypes?'"

Karen slid up to rest her back against the desk, still facing the opposite wall. Walter's legs dangled bear her left shoulder. "Oh, yeah. Like you wouldn't believe how often it comes up when you're sharing a joint with a stage builder at community theater rehearsal."

"You're still involved with the theater?"

"No, but, don't you know that already?"

"Well, yes, obviously. But indulge me. It's more fun that way. Should I continue?"

"Oh, God. Please do."

"Cute" Walter said.

He kicked one foot out toward the wall, turning it into a humongous chalkboard filled with equations and chemical diagrams, perpetually drawing themselves for what looked like miles, well beyond Karen's vision.

"It turns out, there's not really an infinite number of anything. There's practically an infinite number of genotypes, but not literally. Kind of how people say a slot machine is 'totally random,' but there's still an algorithm that governs it. Again, for all intents and purposes, it's random, but go macro enough, and it isn't."

The far end of the chalkboard sucked back toward the center of the room like a tape measure blade, stopping when it made the room square again. "Are you with me so far?"

"Uh, yeah, I guess."

"Karen, you're a smart woman. Don't play dumb."

"You said—"

Walter appeared directly in front of her, sitting cross-legged on the floor. He held up his left hand.

"Anyway. The gateway, the tear in space that your" Walter made air-quotes. "superiors sent you through...by the by, I've always hated it when you all refer to each other as superior or inferior or subordinate. You're literally almost all exactly the same. Almost completely biologically indistinguishable, which, ties in to how we got to where we are now. So, the gate, Bravo 42. It's a selectively permeable membrane; expected, i.e. dead, human genotypes can come in, and they're logged in the system. Those recorded genotypes are allowed to be here, so the security protocols ignore them.

Others, like your mother's pilot friends are discorporated, and their genome packets are added to the system rather abruptly. Unfortunately, like I said, there's not an infinite number of genotypes, so, sometimes, they get repeated. In super rare instances, two repeated genotypes will meet, and produce offspring" he tapped Karen's helmet visor. "the genome repeats are where all that past-life regression nonsense kind of comes from. But, to be fair, I never expected you guys to stumble in here; otherwise, I'd have probably made the protocols way more specific. Now, your mother and father both have genotype combinations that allows you both to pass in and out of the space, so—"

Karen's hand shot up in the air. "You don't have to raise your hand. You're not in class."

"Kinda feels like I am."

"Karen, I know you understand everything that I'm saying."

"Yeah, on like a nuts-and-bolts level, I'm following. But, the thing is, I was kinda expecting a more why I'm here, instead of a how I'm here. Actually, more to the point, why is this here? Why are you here? What's the point of" she waved her hand around the office "this. All of it. Any of it?"

"Your mother told you, didn't she?"

"We don't talk much."

Walter looked surprised.

"You look surprised."

"Me? Surprised? Of course not. I just—anyway; so, like I told Katherine, on one of her incursions here—I am, above all things, a scientist. I make things" just as the last syllable of 'things' left his face, the wall projected a massive explosion in a black void. Gradually, the cosmic debris animated into stars, planets, quasars—you get the idea.

"I watch them. How they interact. Sometimes, when things get stagnant, I give them a little nudge one way or another." The image zoomed through the atmosphere of one of the planets, first revealing microorganisms that turned into proto-mammals, then old world monkeys, then great apes, then a still image of a young Karen attempting to play the trombone.

"I always want to improve the things I make. Most of the way I do that is through intense data collection." The image of Karen zoomed tight to her right eye.

"You ever stop to think about how amazing your eyes are? Not to pat myself on the back or anything, but just think about it. A set of binocular, three dimensional-input high definition cameras made out of water and meat."

The image zoomed through her eye, up her optic nerve, then into her grey matter.

"Transmitting all that data to a lump of fat and water that can hold a million gigabytes of information. Indefinitely. Even if you can't access it, it's always there, and it doesn't finish recording until you drop dead. From your silly little chimp heads," the image snap-zoomed from the brain matter, back out of the eye, the earth, then back to the ordinary wall. "right back to here, carried away from your corpses on gravitational waves."

Karen leaned in until her helmet nearly touched Walter's head.

"Are you telling me that the afterlife is a *fucking* filing cabinet?"

"Well, when you put it that way, it sounds...reductive. But essentially, yes. Again, though, I assumed your mother had told you all of that."

"I told y—"

"I know, I know" he sighed. "Katherine, how long are you going to let this go on?" He reached out and rapped on Karen's helmet with his knuckles.

"Wh—"

MAJOR—Karen. I can explain.

23. Imachination

User.mas;kell ZDD.Danvers PLS uploader
Version 1.3 - September 2097 '--
-------------' Option Explicit Upload/neural_batch 2435632
complete   neural_batch 2435633 complete w/errors;
continue y/n
        y
        neural_batches 2435633;2516781 36% complete
Bind to Active Directory/Mason.PLS.bin Set objRoot=
GetObject/Mason.PLS.dir
Directory:
dir/keller.kar
    keller.kar:0-6
    keller.kar:6-12
    keller.kar:12-18
    keller.kar:18-24
dir/keller.kar:18-24
    state.record:18-24
    federal.record:18-24
    nsa.record.spec:18-24
    medical.record:18-24
    other.record

federal.record:24 object/upload
    object/upload:

<value><text> The President of the United States,
<paragraph>To: Ms. Karen Ernest KELLER 2236-B Ten Apple
Drive, Telluride, CO, 81435 <paragraph/leftjustify> Greetings,

<paragraph/leftjustify>You are hereby ordered for induction into the Armed Forces of the United States, and to report at 1715 REPUBLIC AVENUE, CORVALLIS, OREGON – 3RD FLOOR on 8 JANUARY at 7:25 am <paragraph/leftjustify> for forwarding to an Armed Forces Induction Station.<end.value>

<form name = USMCNASA/ADMIN.dir>
ENTER USER NAME <input type="text" name="mas;kell"> ENTER PASSWORD <input type="password" name="CELFIST">
<input type="button" value="Check In" name="Submit" onclick= "validate()">utilities/processing

C >upload.schedule
schedule: draft.notice/keller.kar.118057037______uploaded to schedule

Directory

dir:
    usmc/medical/colorado/dir

dir/usmcm/col:
    usmcm/col/locations
    usmcm/col/programs
    usmcm/col/finance
    usmcm/col/roster
    <interrupted by user>

dir/usmcm/col/locations
    usmcm/col/loc/denver
    usmcm/col/loc/aurora
    usmcm/col/loc/coloradosprings

dir/usmcm/col/loc/colradosprings
    usmcm/coloradosprings/roster
    usmcm/coloradosprings/finance
    usmcm/coloradosprings/scheduling
    usmcm/coloradosprings/code_ultra

usmcm/coloradosprings/scheduling
    assign/exam_tissue_hair_samples/keller.kar

err:syntax: social
    assign/exam_tissue_hair_samples/keller.kar.118057037

err:syntax: date_time
    assign/exam_tissue_hair_samples_19_09_2097_1400h/kelle
r.kar.118057037

err:dbl_sched
override_schedule/mas;kell:priority_black
assigned:
assign/exam_tissue_hair_samples_19_09_2097_1400h/keller.ka
r.118057037
usmcnasa/logs/technician/ragolia_nathan_spec_27_6_2097
C > del
err:incomplete
del:usmcnasa/logs/technician/ragolia_nathan_spec_27_6_2097
err: del_from
usmcnasa/logs/technician/ragolia_nathan_spec_27_6_2097_cut
_fromtxt/pgph3_according

del:
    <value> <timecode 27_6_2097_2000h>
        <value> <text> to the PLS record, it appears that at some point (a point impossible to determine due to the mechanical issues listed in the previous notes) Captain Mason-Keller encountered, or believes that she encountered, a non-human entity that claimed to be the creator of the Earth and our solar system. We are unable to corroborate this, as there are no audio recordings indicating a presence other than Mason-Keller's, save the 'go home' clip; which we're not certain is a voice at all. We've sent a request to Colonel Morrison to have that audio sample verified by Quantico. She said she'll try to get it pushed

through, but like everything else with this thing, it's a total crapshoot on whether or not there's anyone with the expertise and the clearance to examine it, so we'll see how it goes.

<paragraph/leftjustify> Although we can't confirm the NHE's existence, what we can reasonably infer from all of the audio logs is that Captain Mason-Keller absolutely believes that there is one, and again, according to the audio logs, that the NHE intends to cause an extinction-level event on the Earth through means yet undetermined. We've synced the captain's vital records with the audio logs, and we've determined that her biometrics are consistent with someone who's telling the truth; although I'm sure a psych eval will be more helpful.<endvalue>

usmcnasa/logs/technician/ragolia_nathan_spec_27_6_2097_add_fromtxt/pgph3_according

add:
<value> <timecode 27_6_2097_2000h>
<value> <text> to the PLS records, we've ascertained that Captain Mason-Keller encountered a non-human entity, during her sojourn to the area beyond the Bravo 42 anomaly. According to the data that were released by the PLS, the NHE is not only willing, but capable of inciting an extinction-level event on earth, through superior technological means; means which the PLS is attempting to decrypt, along with our systems. In addition, the sample reports from the Warfighting laboratory indicate that they are rife with a highly dangerous radioactive property to which we are yet unfamiliar.

The PLS has also indicated that the NHE, by its own admission, may be responsible for the erratic weather system that caused the Category-Five Hurricane that crushed Atlanta in June. The most recent audio log we were able to recover has what appears to be the 'voice' of the NHE threatening further destruction if "we refuse to acquiesce to its demands."
<endvalue>

upload/neural_batch/ 2516781complete
    all neural_batches complete, with errors:continue y/n
    y
    warning:if y, batches cannot be overwritten, nor restored to
the source:continue y/n
    y
neural_upload complete

24. Shall not the Landlord of all the Earth do what is Right?

"You have got to be shitting me."

Karen, trust me. I can explain.

"Yeah, you mentioned that; yet still I have a hard time believing it" Karen, rooted to the floor, looked at Walter. He smiled and waved. "Go on, I'll wait" he said. "This is going to be tremendous."

Karen. Sweetheart. Don't listen to this—this thing. I'm your mother.

"Pause."

You can't actually pause me. That was just fo—

"Shut the fuck up a second, will you? I have questions. A lot of them."

We don't really have time for that.

"Hey, Walt? Do we have time? Is time actually a factor here?"

Walter lifted a hand with the fingers pointed straight out, tilting it from side-to-side.

"Helpful. So, Mom. Are you at Lamoni? Did they decide you'd learned your lesson from all of the kid-torching? Have you been listening the whole time?"

Karen, it's not what you think it is. I'm still in Colorado. Physically. But I'm also here. Well, mostly. Here with you. Here for you. You don't know how proud I am of you—everything it took for you to get to where you are now. You really have no idea.

"Bullshit."

Excuse me?

"I said *bbuuuuuullllshiiitt*. You're not proud of me. You've never been proud of anything but you. 'I'm Katherine Mason-Keller, and I'm the greatest pilot in the world' you think I didn't hear that shit? You think I didn't wake up to your fuckin' polyglot babbling and not at least look it up?"

Kar—

"Pipe down, I've got a ways to go. You think I didn't notice there aren't any pictures of me, or dad, anywhere in that whole goddamned house? Just your stupid fucking medals! Well, fat lot of good those did you! Shit, I mean, how hard was it to get those things anyway? You dedicated your whole motherfucking life to that shit, I dedicated mine to toasted sandwiches and open mics, and guess what? We ended up in the same place"

Karen jumped up and down to punctuate the spaces between 'in the same place'.

"Shit, not even. I'm *actually* here, and you're...well I still don't know exactly what your deal is."

My consciousness, such as it is, was integrated into the PLS system.

"Holy shit, seriously?"

It's somewhat more complicated than that, Karen. The neural upload process is—

"Fuck me running. You *did* do it. You're so attached to your fucking job that when they wouldn't let you do it any more, you had yourself turned into fucking office supplies. That's so you."

Karen, you don't—

"No, you don't. Just don't! There's nothing you can say to me that—"

Walter is going to destroy humanity.

"The fuck? Walt, are you going to kill us?"

Walter stood up and extended a hand to Karen. "C'mon, kiddo. Let's go for a walk."

"Whoa. I'm not going anywhere wi—"

Good girl, Karen. You st—

"If you don't shut. The. Fuck. Up. I'll make Walt turn you off again. You can listen, and if I need something, I'll ask. Otherwise, cool your pies. Understood?"

Yes.

"Great. Glad we've got that squared away. As for you," Karen said, standing up to look Walter in the eyes "are you going to blow up the Earth? Can you even do that?"

"Walk with me, Karen."

"I don't..." was all she managed to get out, before she unwillingly rose to her feet.

Walter, now clad in an identical PLS suit to hers, took her hand. The office wall disappeared, revealing a long, grass pathway. On either side of the path were images of human events. Between moving murals of history, they walked.

"Karen, I'm bored…" Walter said. "I've been at it with Earth for, what, four-and-a-half billion years?"

"Uh, sounds about right."

"And I've been at it with humans, like end-model humans, for almost a quarter-million. And you know what I've found?"

"A surprising amount of ingenuity and stick-to-itiveness?"

"Well, that" Walter laughed as they paused beside a collage of images of factories, laboratories, and a picture that Karen recognized as the aftermath of a particularly brutal cluster-bombing of Montreal. "but mostly? I've learned that you guys don't change. Not much."

The industrial and medical images stayed static, while the Montreal image perpetually morphed into various mementos of atrocity. "I mean, from *homo habilis* to *homo sapiens*; huge, massive changes. Tools, culture, religion, entertainment-as different from one another as chimps from fish. Amazing."

"Thanks?"

"Don't mention it. But then, damn near a full stop. You guys could have done literally *anything* you wanted, yet you couldn't get out of your own way. Little spikes, here and there, but mostly nothing. The outfits change, but the song remains the same."

"So?"

An ornate wooden bench rose up to the back of their knees, and they both plopped down. The mural turned into a panoramic shot of what had to be billions of people of every conceivable sex, age, and ethnicity, standing shoulder to shoulder. "So, like I said—I'm bored. I've learned everything about your kind" the billions of people all snapped into a reflection of Karen on the bench "and I want to start over."

I told you so, Karen.

"So you're just going to kill all of us? Just like that?"

"Honestly? I've been contemplating it for a while. I just thought you guys would kind of, ah, take care of it yourselves. Like with climate change, at the turn of the century" he held his left thumb and forefinger a quarter-inch apart "...tthhhiiiiiss close."

Karen jumped to her feet, pointing at the still-seated Walter. "Yeah, but guess what? We all got our shit together, got off fossil fuels, mostly, started recycling more, and we saved ourselves! Weren't you surprised by that?" she asked, jabbing him in the chest with her index finger.

"Not really. And those things you mentioned, those half-measures, weren't the real reason. You all were mostly saved by some completely unexpected, totally chance weather pattern shifts. You have to understand, kiddo, humanity's been surviving almost completely by accident for a couple hundred years. It's like watching someone win a hundred coin tosses in a row. It's interesting, but not scientifically relevant."

"So, that's it."

"Afraid so. But you guys had a good run! In fact, I'm going to keep your genotype around, so whatever I start over with, you'll be part of it!"

"Great."

"It is, even if it doesn't seem like it right now" he said, standing up to rub her on the top of the helmet.

"I'm going to give you some alone time, and you let me know when you're ready to go back. It'll still be a little while before the big" Walter made a throat-slash gesture with his index finger, then disappeared.

I'm so sorry, Karen. I told you what he had planned.

"Ah, so fucking what" Karen answered, flopping down to the grass, hitting her back on the edge of the bench. "Fuck it!" she yelled.

So what, is, there's something you can still do about it. It's the whole reason you're here.

"What?"

You're not here by accident, Karen. I've put everything in position to put you here, right at this moment, so you can complete the mission.

"Oh, I don't think Walt's going to let us build a fucking barracks here, mom."

Karen, on the Craft, there are two ordnance payloads, sufficient to vaporize the entirety of Bravo 42. I need you to arm them. We tested some materials that we brought back with us, and we determined that we are more than capable of neutralizing this place. As for the NH—Walter, we're not sure what it is capable of, but we're not going to risk finding out.

"Bombs?"

You have to be quiet. Walter isn't able to hear me, or sense technology in any useful way. That's why the ships made it in and out unharmed. It's also why I uploaded into the PLS.

"How does he not already know about this?"

The only two people who knew about the operation in full have been placed in medically-induced comas. Barring an accident, there's no way they'll die prior to you completing the mission.

"Why don't you just do it?"

After the Montreal incident, all major ordnance was retrofitted to be incompatible with PLS auto drops. Besides, you need to grow up, and I know you can. You can do this.

"And you want me to, to—that? But I'll, uh, go too, right?"

Unfortunately, but isn't it better to go in a noble pursuit, than to pass out and hit your head on the coffee table, or however you'd expire otherwise.

"Oh, thanks. That's certainly inspiring."

You don't need inspiration. You're fucking Karen Ernest Keller, and you are my daughter. Part of what made me is in you. Despite whatever counter-programming you inherited from your father, you're still half Mason. You have a duty, not just to the Corps; which you're part of, whether you like it or not, but to humanity in general. For once, be a good steward to your fellow man. Be in charge of your destiny. Be in charge of something. Anything.

Spaceship Mase may not have thought that Karen needed inspiration, and she certainly didn't mean for the speech to inspire her the way it did, but, like she said, dynamism wasn't her strong suit.

"Walter?"

Karen! You have to get back to—

Karen grabbed the bottom of the helmet with both hands, wrenching it sharply to the left. The sudden movement broke the vacuum clamp with a satisfying pop. Karen grinned, and threw it as hard as she could, toward the end of the meadow. She felt a tap on her shoulder, and turned to see Walter. He was dressed like a flight attendant.

"Ready to motor, scooter?"

"Not quite. Can I ask you something?"

"Shoot."

"You're bored, right? But you want to start over, and make something new, right? Why can't we stay where we are, and you can just start somewhere else?"

"I wish, kiddo, I really do. But omnipotence isn't quite as infinite as you'd think. I really can't leave you guys unattended. It's irresponsible. What if you guys ruin whatever I move on to?"

"I figured as much" Karen said. "Did you really mean what you said about us being able to do *literally* anything?"

"I sure did, kiddo. You guys are my whole heart. I expected more."

Karen reached out with both hands, and clasped Walter's shoulders. "So, let me do it."

"Do what?"

"Let me take over. For you. You can make that happen, right?"

Walter arched an eyebrow and grinned. "You want me to make you God?"

"No, not really. Just like a.." she fumbled for the word. "...a superintendent."

Walter cocked his head to the side. "You want to be the landlord of the Earth?"

"Yeah" she smiled. "I do. It'll be like a fixer-upper. I can hold down the fort, maybe fix up your security system. All that good shit. So that way, if you ever want to take back over, or just visit or whatever, you can. I'm sure you can swing that for me, right? I mean, you made all this shit" she said, waving vaguely around her.

Walter laughed, not unlike his 'are we special' laugh, but this time, it made Karen feel at ease.

"Karen Keller, you got it. You mind the shop, and I'll go off and do what I do. But, I gotta warn you, it gets pretty boring."

"I think you're underestimating my tolerance for boredom."

"I think I might be." Walter said. He scrunched his face for a second, then relaxed it. "There you go, pal. You're in charge. I'm out of here." He started to fade away.

"Hey, wait a minute."

"What's up?"

"Can you send the ship back, before you bail?"

He laughed again, fading away completely, but his voice hung in the air.

"No, but you can. You can send it anywhere you want! You're the boss!"

And that's how Major Karen Ernest Keller, daughter of Katherine Louise Mason-Keller and Ernest Jerome Keller became Karen Keller, superintendent of Earth.

So, if you need anything, just contact her at

Karen,
Superintendent of Earth
Bravo 42 Anomaly

<u>About the Author</u>

R. N. Jorden is kind to animals and can dance the tango at a championship level. Jorden's got tactical smart missiles, phased plasma pulse rifles, RPGs, sonic electronic ball breakers, nukes, knives, and sharp sticks. Jorden currently resides in Hadley's Hope.

Amanda Hardebeck has been a sci-fi & film addict since birth. When her older brother handed her a copy of *Dune* for her birthday 20 years ago, her passion for science fiction took off. She is a roller derby referee for her hometown team and is Chief Editor for Spaceboy Books LLC.

TJ Stambaugh received several commendations for his bravery as a battalion commander in the Meme Wars. After the war, TJ retired to Catonsville, MD, where he paints, enjoys movies you have to read, and is Art Director for Spaceboy Books LLC.

Learn more about Spaceboy Books at readspaceboy.com